FIRWOOD

The Magic Garden

Written By

LYNNE ARMSTRONG-HOBBS

First published in Great Britain in 2010 by Lynne Armstrong-Hobbs

Copyright © Lynne Armstrong-Hobbs 2010

The publisher has asserted her moral rights to be identified as the author.

A CIP Catalogue of this book is available from the British Library

ISBN: 978-0-9565211-0-1

Cover designed and typeset in Fairfield 11½pt
by Chandler Book Design
www.chandlerbookdesign.co.uk

Illustrated by Sue Navin

Printed in Great Britain by the
MPG Books Group, Bodmin and King's Lynn

For Holly and Victoria
who make every day magical

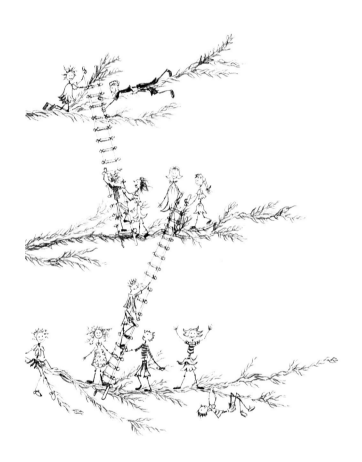

Contents

List of Illustrations

Chapter One

The Magic Garden

Long ago – in fact thousands upon thousands of years ago - a small piece of the moon dropped out of the sky and fell to Earth. As luck would have it, it landed in an everyday garden and changed it forever! All of the exciting adventures that you will read about happened in this garden, which became highly magical as a result of this moon piece.

Nobody saw it land on that dark, rainy night, or knew that it was buried deep in the ground by the sheer force of its landing.

Well, no one, that is, except the animals who already lived there - and one evil Thworg who happened to be close by at the time.

So just outside the little market town of Cirencester, where the road turns sharply to the right and winds eastwards out of the town, the magic garden is hidden,

1

tucked away from the hustle and bustle of the world. Here, opposite a tranquil field where people tend to their vegetables, our story begins. For directly across the road from these allotments, two large stone pillars announce the beginning of a garden - and here is Firwood, the most magical and secret garden in England!

Monty and the animals of Firwood

Monty surveyed the garden from his seating-place on a square stone tub, his bright emerald eyes gleaming in the sunlight. A tabby cat of remarkable markings, he was a handsome cat who made his owners proud. What they did not know was that Monty was also the cat-guardian of the magic garden, and that the animals who lived there were also proud of their leader and held him in great respect.

Monty sat tall looking straight ahead; he could see the rich green grass as it sloped gently down to the round flowerbed at the front of the grounds. The flowerbed with its tall plants and bushes, protected the core of the garden's magic: at its very centre, the moonpiece was kept in what the animals called the Ennyl.

The Ennyl itself was an extremely old stone plant-pot, which was defined by tiny markings all around it. Some

of the animals said that this was the writing of a lost language, but even the field mice who could peer closely into the tiny crevices were unable to decipher it. They said it changed, and that the markings moved if they returned to where they had looked before. It was all very mysterious. However, it was accepted by the animals of Firwood, as was often necessary in the garden that some things do not need to be fully understood.

As Monty gazed at a tree past the flowerbed where the fine, wispy ends made it look as though little puffs of smoke were being blown from its top, he became aware of a commotion to his right. He turned a pointy ear towards the noise and the other side of the garden, from which he heard the unmistakable bark of the small black poodle from next door.

'Dogs!' Monty sighed to himself, as he jumped down from the tub and ambled towards Sooty the poodle. Sooty is in for a bit of a shock, he thought, since he's never been inside the magic garden before!

But wait! Before I can continue, I must let you know an important fact about Firwood's magic garden, for all of the animals who lived in the garden could speak; not just to each other, but to humans, too! That is how the children who lived in the house, Holly and Victoria, got to know them all, and could also join in their adventures.

Indeed Sooty, the black poodle who lived next door, was shocked when he jumped over the fence! One minute he was barking at a blackbird in the pine tree, the next being shouted at to 'watch out!' by Barry and Claudia, the twin squirrels, as he landed in Firwood after his daredevil leap.

To Sooty's own astonishment he heard himself say, 'Oh, sorry! I didn't mean to nearly land on you!' in the most perfect human language. Jumping backwards and tripping over his own back legs at the shock that he too could speak, he looked very funny indeed; at which point the squirrels and Sooty himself burst out laughing.

'You live next door, don't you?' said Claudia, the larger of the twins, as she stripped a beech nut of its outer case with her long nimble fingers and began to nibble at it.

'Yes,' said Sooty rather bemusedly, as he was still trying to come to terms with the fact that not only could he speak, but all of the animals in this garden seemed to be able to! Two small grey field mice had just scooted past in a hurry shouting 'Hi! Lovely day for a paddle!' and Sooty watched as they gingerly dipped their feet into a very large puddle before beginning to sail tiny green leaves like little boats, racing from one side of the murky water to the other. (There is much more, of course, to this land of enchantment than talking animals, but you will find this all out in time.)

Monty, bounding across the grass, arrived at the spot that Sooty had landed in just in time to explain to him all about Firwood and its magic. From that moment on, Sooty and Monty were great friends. In fact, Sooty's owners spent many days trying to retrieve him from next door's garden, as well as wondering why he spent so much time playing with the cat who lived there in a very un-dog-like manner!

Beneath the garden and deep into the earth, the blue treeglies had their own world. They were very rarely seen, but if they were in the garden all of the animals sensed it. The blue treeglies were half-moons of blue light, like tiny fluorescent tubes, all exactly the same. They rose from the grass and disappeared again very quickly, as if they were swimming like dolphins through the ocean, graceful and unhindered. Sometimes, they glided this way and that across the garden; and if they did appear, on those very rare occasions, only Monty and a handful of other animals were ever quick enough to see them. However, all the animals felt the presence of the blue treeglies when they were around. A warm glow would fill the garden, and funny things would happen! They, too, it seemed were guardians of this special place.

And so the animals of Firwood and the blue treeglies lived in undisturbed harmony... until, of course, another adventure began!

Chapter Two

Wampum

Today was a day of excitement. The biggest celebration of the year was about to take place; tomorrow evening was Wampum. This was a gathering of not only all those who lived in the garden, but relatives and friends, who would travel for days to join in the fun and see for themselves the wonderment. It was rumoured that this marked the exact day that, long ago, the piece of the moon had landed here.

Piggling had begun in earnest a week before. The guinea pigs, of the long-haired variety, had begun this ritual. Each morning at 10am they would emerge from their home, a pretty wooden hutch, down the long plank that led to the grass below, and here they began to 'piggle.' Their tiny pale pink snouts glued to the ground, they moved with feet that had been preened and readied for their task. Cinnamon and Treacle were brothers, and both very much alike with grey, white and yellowish patches of hair.

Each fifteen minute 'piggling' session, which was like a dance, had over a hundred elaborate steps of trumpery and flashery that would take the breath away of any animal observer. This piggling dance had been passed carefully down from parent to child for generations, right back to their ancestors who had lived in China. Of course, to humans, this would look like the innocent grazing of two domestic guinea pigs... but then what did they know? The festival of Wampum could not begin until the guinea pig dance had been danced!

Darkness had fallen across the garden and so the visiting animals began to emerge. They had hidden in the hedges, bushes and trees leading to Firwood. They began to march up the drive and find themselves a good spot on the grass to enjoy the spectacle. There were families of tiny moles, rabbits, splendid large hares, hopping toads and the very beautiful blue-green dragonflies who flew across the hedges. In and around the branches of the trees wood pigeons, robins and woodpeckers swooped onto the lawn and got comfortable, many greeting or joining old friends.

Earlier that day, Monty had spoken to Holly and Victoria, who lived in the house that the garden belonged to. The girls were very keen to see the festival, but sneaking out of the house after their parents were asleep was going to be tricky. The children had always stroked and petted Monty, but got quite a surprise when one day last summer he spoke to them in the garden and told them all about how special the garden was.

Monty revealed that the animals within the garden could talk, but also urged them to keep this revelation a secret; the garden's magic must be protected at all costs. Since then, Holly and Victoria had met and made friends with lots of other animals who lived in the garden too. The girls had heard lots of talk about the Wampum festival and were very excited to see it.

Midnight approached. The moon was full, large and bright. It was hidden, glimpsed, then hidden again, by a thick white curtain of fluffy clouds that seemed to fill the dark evening sky.

Holly and Victoria carefully unlocked the heavy wooden front door of the house. They gasped as they saw

what seemed like a blanket of animals, of all different shapes and sizes, sitting on every part of their vast lawn. They were all facing the flowerbed in the middle of the front lawn, and, at its centre, the ancient stone urn, which they had heard the animals call the 'Ennyl.'

'How beautiful the garden looks!' said Holly, whispering excitedly to her sister. The trees shimmered with gold and silver. Their trunks had been painted by the animals for this special occasion, and they were decorated with an array of baubles and ornaments made from leaves and red berries, which were threaded together and hanging from branch to branch. Shiny jewels too festooned the bottom half of the tree trunks: rubies, creamy white pearls, and shimmering diamonds. They were quite stunning and polished to perfection. Suddenly, a voice whispered, 'This way, children!'

Barbara, one of the three wood pigeons who lived in the tall green fir trees, was right beside them.

'Follow me!' and she led them to a space in front of the stone tub. Here, a rug had been placed for them to sit on.

The air felt electric, as if something tremendous was about to happen. And indeed it was, for without warning, midnight arrived.

A soft warm breeze began to blow. Everyone gasped as the sky above them suddenly cleared; it was as if a giant hand had lent across the moon's path, pulling aside the curtain of little white clouds and revealing the moon: majestic, huge, and especially bright on this most special of evenings.

Victoria squeezed Holly's arm. They were both transfixed. The garden fell silent as the chattering of the animals stopped.

Next, a sliding sound from the centre of the garden reverberated as the stone urn, the Ennyl, unfolded like the petals of a flower. Everyone gasped, for as the Ennyl opened, a beam of sparkling light flooded from the moon into the centre of the urn, bathing it in a continuous ribbon of silver. The children did not know it at the time, but the moon was Cousin to the earth, Uncle to the blue treeglies, and a most sacred treasure was kept at the centre of this magical garden: a piece of the moon itself!

Glittering pale yellow stars appeared, spinning around the base of the moon, weaving an intricate pattern beneath it.

Then a noise, like the crack of a whip, made the girls jump. The most fantastic fountain of blue treeglies burst forth from the centre of the Ennyl. A cheer went up from the animals as these beautiful creatures filled the sky, rising and dropping, spinning and looping, higher and higher: a giant firework of blue treeglies, stretching up to the sky, higher than the house, and three times higher again, up and up as if they would never stop.

The dazzled audience followed the music of their movement and felt a calmness, then a glow of happiness and hope. Even the girls felt that for a moment all the inhabitants of the garden had been transported to another world.

Then, without warning and as if awakening from a dream, everything returned to as it had been before. The Ennyl had closed and the sky was no longer filled with blue treeglies, all, it seemed, within less than a second, as if time had momentarily been suspended.

Music began to play softly and picnic baskets were opened, as a party began in the magic garden. The animals began to laugh and talk. Holly and Victoria still gazed skyward for a few more minutes, just to take in what had just happened.

The energy of the moon had filled the Ennyl: why? And what were the secrets within it? The children now had lots of questions that they were desperate to ask Monty and the others.

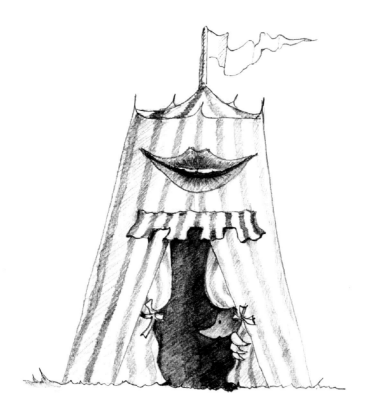

Chapter Three

Madame Mole & The Giant Snowflakes

Just then Monty joined the children. Holly noticed that on this special evening of Wampum he had a look of great pride.

'Come and meet one of our colourful guests,' he said.

The children stood up and followed him. A small, striped, pink and purple round tent had been erected at the back of the garden; it was barely the size of Victoria's doll house. 'Madame Mole,' announced a big painted red mouth at the entrance.

'All questions answered, the future foretold,' the mouth continued, followed by a welcoming smile.

'Madame Mole is known for her ability to see into the future,' whispered Monty, as they all walked towards the tent.

'Please meet and greet our honored guests, Holly

17

and Victoria, the children who live in Firwood House,' he then announced, as they approached the entrance.

'How wonderful to meet you girls; do come inside!' said Madame Mole, in a squeaky sing-song voice. Just as Holly was about to apologise and explain that the size of the tent would make this impossible, they found themselves entering as if by magic.

There was a pinkish glow inside. A thick gold chain, joined to posts, formed a circle inside the tent; it was hung with lanterns and jugs of all shapes and sizes - and, surprisingly, the odd mobile telephone.

'Do please sit!' said Madame Mole, gesturing to the large oriental cushions scattered on the floor. Both girls happily sank into this most comfortable seating arrangement. Giant feathers lent against the walls of the tent, some bigger than the girls themselves: thick and lavish feathers, all colours imaginable, giving a snug feeling to the inside of the tent.

'Ah,' said Madame Mole, watching their reaction, 'I can see you like my feathers.'

Madame Mole was extremely dainty; her tiny feet held graciously in front of her, she smiled and chatted to the children. She was an amazing story-teller, and everyone settled down to listen to her as she span her many tales. The girls listened intently, drinking the delicious raspberry and petal juice they were given.

The party outside was getting louder, and soon Monty suggested they join it, so as not to miss the spectacle of the snow.

'More surprises, Monty,' said Vikki, smiling as she lent over and stroked him gently on his back.

'Meow,' said Monty with a wink and they all giggled.

As they were leaving the tent, they were each presented with a feather from Madame Mole. Holly's was a soft pale blue, and Victoria's a fiery orange.

'These penfeathers may help you in the future: if you write wisely, you shall see me again,' she said in a voice that faded as she disappeared into her tent. At the same time, the children were suddenly outside of it.

Before they had chance to say even one word to each other, it began to snow. This was not like any snow that they had ever witnessed before, for the snowflakes were three times the size. As the girls looked upwards they couldn't help but laugh; the giant flakes tickled their faces. They both looked so funny to each other, covered so quickly from head to foot in white; they kept having to blink to clear their eyes. The animals round about were like moving snow sculptures, and soon the garden was completely white.

Snowball fights were happening all around them,

and some of the animals formed little groups to make snow squirrels and snow cats and snow mice! not a snow man in sight.

'Let's not miss the ice-boarding,' said Monty, ducking as a snowball came whizzing towards him.

'Quick, back to the front garden!' The girls slipped and slid as they tried to keep up with Monty, who looked very different as a completely white fluffy cat with snowy white whiskers.

'I'm not even cold!' shouted Holly as they rounded the house.

'The raspberry and petal drinks!' Monty shouted back.

At the front of the house, lining the winding drive, were the three holly trees,: two of them tall, with a mass of spiky pea-green leaves and topped with red berries, next to them the short fat one, half the size but just as wide, standing like a lollipop of green and yellow leaves.

A steep hill of snow had appeared alongside these holly trees and sledges of squirrels sped down. Once they had arrived at the bottom, they would race back round to climb up again and slide as fast as they could once again, this time some of them standing rather than sitting! There was a lot of laughter and squealing as animals tumbled down occasionally bumping into each other, forming little clumps of paws and legs sticking out of the snow.

All sorts of things were in use by the smaller animals. Several mice slid down in a plastic flower pot.

Monty jumped onto a flat piece of wood and was gone, sliding in the distance!

'Come on!' he shouted.

'This is too good to miss!' said Victoria whose eyes were wide with excitement. There were a pile of cushions that looked remarkably like the ones in Madame Mole's tent; grabbing one each, the girls shot down the hill. Again and again they slid.

'Cool!' shouted Holly, as Monty sped past on - of all things - a yellow frisbee.

After a while, Victoria realised her legs were beginning to ache and she was feeling very tired.

Holly plopped down beside her. 'You look shattered, Vic, and I am too. Just time for one last slide!'

Meeting Sooty and Monty at the top of the hill, all four of them slid down together, cheering as they whooshed to the bottom. Then the girls said goodnight to everyone, and Sooty the little black poodle guided them back to their front door.

'Eat this,' he said, handing each of them a giant mauve flower as big as an apple but shaped like a giant daisy. 'Tacs, they are delicious of course.' He wiggled his nose mischievously. 'But best of all you will feel completely refreshed.'

The girls both ate the tacs straight away, as they suddenly realised they were very hungry.

'Oooh, yum!' said Holly, 'They taste like strawberry ice cream!'

'With syrup on!' mumbled Victoria, as she savored the rest in her mouth.

Sneaking quietly into the house, they climbed into their beds feeling very content, and not at all hungry anymore. They fell immediately into a lovely sleep, clutching their new penfeathers.

Chapter Four

Hedgehogs In Danger

Many weeks passed when the girls had not had chance to spend time in the garden with the animals because of their schoolwork. By the time they got home from school it was always too dark and cold to go outside. Imagine their excitement at the beginning of the summer holidays: now they would have all the time in the world to spend in the magical garden again!

On the first sunny day of their holidays, Holly and Victoria invited their friend Tom to play, hoping secretly that they would be able to show him the garden's secret wonders. Of course, they would never do so without Monty's permission; he was, after all, the garden's official guardian. Victoria approached him as he was stretched out across the living room sofa, looking very content and just like any other cat.

Victoria cuddled close to him and began to explain – with her voice almost at a whisper – about their hopes for Tom to see the garden as they had seen it, though he could talk in the garden Monty could not speak inside the house and so he beckoned them outside and purred as he rubbed against the children's legs. Then he spoke to them 'Tom will be welcome,' he assured them to their delight, 'but I must remind you to never speak freely about the garden to anyone without my permission. We do have enemies.' He lowered his voice, and continued. 'The moonpiece that is protected here is sought by others, who would steal it away if they could.'

'But who and why?' whispered Vikki, intrigued.

Monty glanced around, and then walked behind the wall at the back of the garden, gesturing to the girls to follow him. Here they were hidden from any prying eyes or ears.

'Thworgs,' he snarled with obvious venom.

Holly felt a shiver through her spine; she had never seen Monty angry before, so the very mention of these terrible creatures must concern him deeply.

However, they didn't have a very long time to dwell over this, as suddenly, without warning, something hit Holly hard on the head.

'Ow!' she cried.

'You can say that again!' said Vikki, as a twig landed

on her, followed by a beech nut.

All three of them heard a tiny mischievous giggle, and then another.

'Right,' said Holly, slowly bending down and picking up a short stick. 'I think I know who it is!'

She quickly threw the stick up into the fir tree, where the giggle had obviously come from. Barry and Claudia the squirrels playfully leapt across to the next tree and down the trunk, hurling small twigs as they did and shouting, 'Join the chase if you dare!'

Holly, Monty and Victoria quickly ran towards the wilder part of the garden, around the back of the house where the grass grew longer and the flowers intertwined. The three then crept quietly around the wall and hid behind the bonfire that sat in the middle of this wilderness.

Sure enough, they soon heard the crackle of wood as two naughty squirrels rushed through the branches of the beech tree and ran swiftly down its trunk again.

'Gotcha!' shouted Holly, and they began to chase Barry and Claudia themselves. Monty leapt in front to head off the twin squirrels, who had to quickly jump and half turn to change direction and avoid being caught. Victoria dashed forward and nearly caught Claudia by her red bushy tail, but she just missed and the squirrels scurried up the smoke tree. Monty sped up after them, as he did, a loud shrill whistling was heard reverberating around the garden, and they all stopped abruptly.

'Cinnamon and Treacle - the warning call – quick!' said Monty, and he and the others ran back down the tree as fast as they could.

The whistling of the guinea pigs continued calling out to all of the animals of Firwood.

Monty soon had them in view, and the wood pigeons with them. He dashed down the drive to join the group of animals, followed by Holly, Victoria, Barry, and Claudia. 'What's your report?' Monty asked Cinnamon, catching his breath.

'A hedgehog - just outside the drive - three houses down to the left,' said Cinnamon urgently, his voice low and serious in tone.

'Injured?' Monty enquired.

'Not... not moving at all, sir,' stammered Treacle, who looked terribly upset; it was always distressing for the animals to see others in danger or hurt.

Monty immediately began to issue orders. 'All animals of the garden stay here except the wood pigeons: you fly around and above to make sure it's all clear.' Then he went to the base of the smoke tree and dug with his front paws furiously. He lifted what looked like a thin leather shoe lace from the mound and placed it around his neck, saying, 'With this I will still be able to talk to you outside the garden, children.' Purposefully, he stalked out of the drive and along the pavement, first passing Sooty's home next door to Firwood and then the houses beyond.

Holly Tom and Victoria went with him. There was, an eerie atmosphere as they walked along the pavement in silence together; dusk was beginning to fall and lent a shadowy look to the hedges lining the road. They were all wondering what they would find.

A flap of wings behind and above them made them start.

'Just us, sir,' trilled Barbara, 'all clear as far as we can see.' So the four friends continued along the pavement.

At first it was difficult to see anything, until Barbara pointed out to them: 'Look there, close to the hedge.'

They all gasped as a shape came into sight; a large hedgehog lay on its side at the edge of the road, eyes closed and its body uncurled. It wasn't moving at all.

Holly bent down to look closer. The hedgehog's slim, black, leathery hands were wrapped tightly together and seemed to be holding something. 'It looks like a note,' she whispered.

'Oh poor thing!' cried Victoria, 'Perhaps it was hit by a car?'

27

Just then, she spotted two smaller shapes only a metre away and, trying to keep back her tears, whispered, 'Oh no...look..' There were two smaller hedgehogs nearby, in the same position as their mother. Monty crept closer and pressed his ear next to their tiny mouths, but he could not hear even the smallest breath. Next, he gently tugged the note from the mother hedgehog with his teeth and read it silently. 'Thworgs - they were trying to escape from thworgs he said, drawing in his breath. He looked angry, but quickly regained his composure.

'We must take them to the magic garden at once,' he continued with urgency. 'Let's make sure we can't be seen; they may have been followed, and could still be being watched. Everyone must be extra careful and alert.' Springing onto a nearby wall, he surveyed the surrounding area before allowing the party to continue back towards Firwood.

'Why on earth would anyone want to harm these poor innocent creatures?' Holly gulped, she felt like crying but didn't.

'Thworgs,' said Monty, quietly, 'have no feelings for other animals. They have been searching for the magic moonpiece in the garden for a very long time; in fact, they would use the energy it draws from the moonbeams to make slaves of all of the animals on earth.'

Holly felt her stomach tighten and a twinge of terror.

'How awful!' she and Victoria cried in unison.

'There's no time to discuss it. We must get back quickly,' Monty replied. Between them they carried the motionless hedgehogs back towards the garden.

Back at Firwood, the other animals were all waiting they stood around the special flowerbed on the front lawn, here Holly, Tom and Victoria solemnly lay the hedgehogs. One by one, each animal began to gently cover the mother and her two babies with leaves gathered from the ground and trees.

Claudia the red squirrel began to cry, large warm tears rolling down her cheeks as she stepped forward and gently placed several green leaves over them.

Holly and Victoria looked very solemn, and eventually Victoria began to ask, 'Are they...?'

But before she could finish, two blue treeglies appeared above them. The treeglies hovered above the flowerbed and then glided over and under the hedgehogs again and again; as if they were wrapping invisible thread around them, the animals and the children felt the familiar warm glow inside that always accompanied a visit from their friends the treeglies. Suddenly, the little blankets of leaves began to move. Everyone held their breath, could it be that the treeglies were able to help the little family, dare they hope?

Monty moved closer to determine what had happened. Immediately he leapt up the trunk of the adjacent tree and announced jubilantly 'The hedgehogs are saved' The blue treeglies swam silently through the air above them, somersaulting and spinning, and then disappeared back down into the earth, having completed their good deed.

As the animals began to realise what had just happened, they started to shout and clap with joy, and an impromptu celebration began. The animals of Firwood love any excuse to have a party!

Pretty lime-green cakes topped with white icing were whipped up in no time by the fieldmice for everyone to share, and the squirrels quickly supplied delicious raspberry and petal juice in empty beech shells.

'Listen,' said Barbara the wood pigeon to Holly and Victoria, and as they did so they recognised the song they heard, which was emanating throughout the garden: it had been sung during the Wampum festival. Together, all the animals of Firwood were singing softly their favourite song:

I went out to the hazelwood
Because a fire was in my head
And cut and peeled a hazel wand
And hooked a berry to a thread

Chapter Five

The Tiny Stick People

Monty explained to the girls and their friend Tom later that evening that Thworgs had always sought the magic of this beautiful place. Now, looking around, the children were aware just how lovely their garden was: seven acres of garden, divided into special 'rooms' filled with such pretty plants and flowers, streams that meandered through the grassy lawns, the little stone bridge linking the poppy garden to the rose garden. The stepping stones and even the view from the east wall were all quite magical. In fact, what should have taken the work of many gardeners to maintain seemed to strangely take care of itself. How dreadful it would be to lose this small paradise to evil Thworgs!

Continuing, Monty told the children that he thought the hedgehogs had been headed for the garden when they had been attacked.

'I believe our little trio will have had to be very brave in order to keep our location secret; our enemies may have tried to make them lead them here.'

'How could the Thworgs convince animals to trust them ever?' said Tom, defiantly.

'Thworgs are very scary, Tom. Once under their power, you are helpless and lost. But one thing they can never change is the icy bitter wind that surrounds them, thank goodness, for it is this very coldness that warns us they are near,' Monty replied, with a shudder. 'Remember, they seek our moonpiece and believe its power is the key that will help them to conquer our world. They thrive only on wickedness.'

Monty got to his feet and the children knew that, for now, this was the end of the discussion.

Walking away from them and towards the hedgehogs, Monty turned and looked back at the girls briefly, saying with authority: 'These Thworgs are not of any animal breed or human kind. Beware of their trickery.'

Monty saw that, though not quite dark, it would be soon; they must hurry to ensure the hedgehogs, weak from their ordeal, could be made warm and safe for the night. Arriving at the spot where the hedgehogs were resting, Monty bent down and spoke to them, he offered a permanent home here in the magic garden.

Hearing Monty's kind words, the mother hedgehog rolled onto her side and then sat up and introduced herself to them. She insisted, after introductions had been made, that it was important for her kind rescuers to know exactly what had occurred.

The animals huddled closer around their new friend Dilly the hedgehog. They sipped warm apple juice and were hushed and quiet as they listened to what had happened to her and her two children.

Still breathless, and in a quiet, gentle voice, she confirmed that they had set off from their own home in the outer wood. The little hedgehogs were excited to see their friends and they were all, of course, very much looking forward to Wampum. The journey would take two days, and so they carried little blue and white spotty bags with games and toys to entertain them and some delicious things to eat; they would have fun on the way, so they thought.

On the morning of the second day, Dilly told the animals, she was aware of a sudden cold breeze; it would settle for a few seconds and then quickly be gone, a bit like walking through a deep freeze and out the other end. Several times she had stopped and, raising herself onto her hind legs and holding her small black snout high, hoped that her keen sense of smell would give her a clue as to what caused it and the uneasy feeling she had.

Another cold wind blasted across the little family as they walked together past the old windmill, which creaked in the wind. It was at this point, by the windmill only a street away from Firwood, that she realised it must be Thworgs and it was likely they had been following them for some time!

Cinnamon and Treacle trembled as they heard this part of the story. Dilly rested for a moment and slowly reached forward to sip more of the warm apple juice to give her strength, then she went on.

'I decided we must fool them and lead them away from the magic garden.' The young hedgehogs squeaked and pressed themselves closer to their mother as they remembered how scared they had been.

'I knew we were close to the stables at Pale Farm, so I changed direction and headed there.'

Holly's mouth fell open and she and Victoria exchanged glances, for this was where their Mum rode horses every week.

'Go on,' said Barbara the kindly wood pigeon to Dilly, encouragingly.

'The little ones were exhausted, so we crawled into an empty horse box of soft yellow straw and slept. At sunrise the next day, I guided the children back to the long country lane; we were all still very tired, but I thought we had lost the Thworgs.

'Nearing the magic garden I began to feel drowsy and exhausted' Click and Clack were struggling to walk. Eventually they just lay down, it was then I knew I must at least try to warn the animals of the garden and quickly scribbled what I could. Before I had time to hide my note under a stone, or in the hedge, I too fell, still clasping the note I had written.

'Dear, brave friend, we are all very grateful to you for protecting our secret. Three times at least you were all exposed to the deathly chill of the Thworgs, so it is little wonder that when we found you, you were already unconscious. Come - you are all clearly very tired.' Monty led the way to the shelter of the three large, tall fir trees. Holly, Victoria, and Tom then watched with astonishment as two extremely long, thick ropes of ivy were dropped from the very top of the fir trees. Looking up, they saw that the tree-tops seemed to merge into one mass of thick green and black. Lots more was happening now, as the

ivy ropes reached the bottom. The ivy was twisted around
a rectangular platform of silver bark, easily big enough to
hold the hedgehogs. A twig fence had been built around
it to protect those it carried. Now it was being expertly
hauled back up to the top of the trees with its precious
cargo of hedgehogs on board.

Once at the top, the hedgehogs found themselves in
a wonderful tree house. There were four wooden beds,
each with a round table and two miniature wooden rocking
chairs. A shiny silver bowl was in the middle of the solid
oak table, full to the brim with nuts and berries to eat.

'Let's sleep now, children,' said Dilly, 'there will be lots of time to explore our new home tomorrow.'

Grabbing a handful of berries and nuts, they each heaved themselves into the pretty wooden beds, which were quite high to little hedgehogs, and while nibbling their fine treat fell fast asleep.

Having watched the bark platform carrying the hedgehogs disappear into the thick green boughs of the fir trees, something else caught the attention of the children, a sudden movement.

'Look!' pointed Tom, laughing, for the tree was suddenly alive with tiny stick people, tumbling from branch to branch. They were only about four inches from head to toe with pink rosy cheeks, bright red lips and blue eyes. Their tiny arms and legs were twigs but moved and bent easily as if made of wire. Each

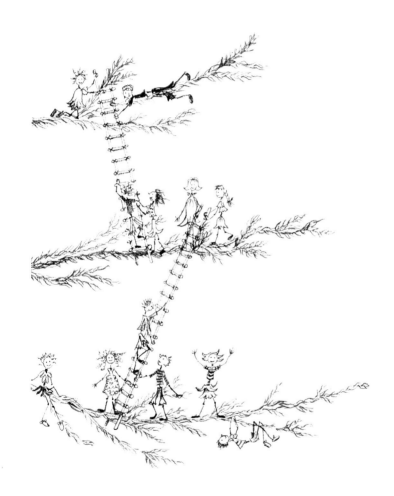

had different coloured hair – twizzled curls of jet black sticking out from their perfectly round wooden heads, or the colour of pale buttery straw and straight. They wore the sweetest clothes.

'Oh!' gasped Holly, as several little stick people climbed down a set of tiny blue and yellow ladders that had appeared from nowhere. Each time, the ladder would then be held again by those at the bottom and dropped further down, as if it were a never ending unfolding structure. There were hundreds of them!

As they got closer to the children and further down the trees, the stick people's faint voices could just be heard. It was now easier to see their clothing, and what a privilege, since the stick people took enormous pride in what they wore! Some had skirts made of daffodils worn upside down or rose petals sewn together; others, miniature wool jumpers of blue and white stripes, or emerald green dresses with the finest matching grass net petticoats and shoes.

As they descended the trees towards the children, they sang their woodland song. So beautiful was the singing that the children were utterly entranced. Holly put out her hand and a stick girl wearing a pink dress that looked like candy floss hopped onto it and smiled up at her. She began to dance on her hand.

Meanwhile, Victoria had sat down on the grass and was happily being pampered by at least twenty little stick people! Six were on her shoulders with tiny combs, combing her long blonde hair; several were dotting little pots of home-made cream on her arms and humming happily.

Tom lay on his tummy and, resting on his elbows, watched the antics of another little group who were playing ball games with freshly picked redcurrants. Just by his shoulder, a few grass mats had been put down and some acrobats proudly somersaulted and vaulted over little carved wooden horses! They were all smiling and happily playing, showing no fear of the children who towered over them at all - until suddenly, the piercing sound of a horn rang out in three long, trill notes.

In response to this, the little stick people began to carefully gather their things and make their way back up the trees in the same manner that they had descended, leaving no trace of themselves, and singing as they went.

'Do come and play again!' the children cried after them, but the little stick people just hummed and sang obliviously as they effortlessly swung themselves back up the tree and were gone.

'Do you know,' said Holly, 'this really is the most incredible garden! What next?'

Chapter Six

Mr Leafblower &
His Leaf Flume

The early afternoon sun was hot and the children sat on the neatly cut lawn stroking Cinnamon and Treacle on a late summer's day. Many weeks had passed without thought of the threat of the terrible Thworgs, and the garden was at peace once again.

As the girls pondered this, Cinnamon and Treacle began to head for the compost heap at the bottom of the garden, where many lush dandelions grew.

Following their friends, Holly and Victoria each picked up a twig from the ground and began to absentmindedly prod at the heap of rotting leaves and vegetables that made up the large compost heap. However, they were quite unnerved by the response! The whole heap suddenly began to move!

'Eek!' shouted Holly, and she grabbed her sister's

arm and pulled her behind the trunk of the nearest tree. 'There's something in there - and it's big, whatever it is!' she whispered to Victoria.

With that the whole thing erupted, cuttings and leaves flying everywhere.

They were both stunned as a rather stout individual heaved himself out of the heap and stood before them. Though he was nearly as tall as them, his round body jutted outwards in all directions. Wearing a jacket made of brown leaves that didn't quite fit, and green leaf trousers that stopped just below his knees, he looked quite funny rather than scary. His sharp, triangular blinking eyes and a half-moon mouth made him look like he had been carved out of a pumpkin.

Victoria began to giggle at the sight of this strange figure, and Holly quickly jabbed her sister in the ribs with a swift move of her elbow.

'He might be offended!' she whispered, glaring at her sister.

Just then, they heard Treacle in his whistling voice say, 'Oh, it's only Mr Leafblower,' before continuing with his lunch. Holly could just see flashes of the snowy white hair of the two guinea pigs as they moved between the tall round dandelion clocks and blades of grass. They clearly knew this person already.

Then a thunderous but very posh voice rang out: 'Jolly well too hot to stay indoors today!' Mr Leafblower held out a hand and introduced himself to each of them in turn, tipping his head forward in a half bow as he did so.

It was Holly who spoke first; although she was a little

shocked, she did not want to appear rude.

'Do you live in the compost heap, Mr Leafblower?' she asked. 'Well, now,' said Mr Leafblower, plonking himself down on the grass and unscrewing a bell-shaped bottle, 'You might say that I do, but', he continued, pushing back his black wavy hair with one hand and tossing his head, 'that really is only the beginning, if you know what I mean.'

Of course the girls did not, and with that he took a very long drink from his bottle and let out a tremendous burp, smiling widely at them.

'Homemade lemonade - my favourite! Now to explain.'

Mr Leafblower beamed at the girls and, blinking several times, continued: 'It is of course true that I live in the compost heap, BUT,' and he held up his broad hand and paused for a long time as if to stop any interruptions that might occur, and then continued, 'that is only my front door, as it were, my tunnel.' And he paused again. 'Of course, it has many homes branching off this way and that,' he finished.

'Oh, Mr Leafblower, you have a tunnel? Can we see it?' cried Victoria, who was always keen to explore.

Cinnamon and Treacle were now full to the brim with their lunches and waddled over to join them. They and Mr Leafblower swapped news and then Cinnamon suggested that it would be great fun to take the girls on the leaf flume.

'Yes, yes!' cried Mr Leafblower, 'Capital idea, capital!' and he did a little dance on the spot, unable to contain his glee.

The girls immediately took to their new friend and without hesitation assured him they would love to see the leaf flume, even though they weren't quite sure what it was.

Delighted, Mr Leafblower stood and, taking big bouncy steps, arrived at the back of the compost heap in seconds; the girls and guinea pigs quickly followed. Here, Mr Leafblower spun round to face them, and began to use his strong back legs to kick aside the leaves and grass cuttings from a particular spot. A small, square door was soon revealed, which seemed to have been woven from the discarded roots and grass.

Holly, Victoria, Cinnamon and Treacle all squeezed inside and followed their new friend as he climbed carefully down a sturdy metal ladder.

'Cool' said Victoria. Looking ahead, they could see they were in the entrance to a magnificent grass den. The inside was dim but still visible, because at least twenty old car headlights were dotted around the floor to provide some light. Then, over to the right, Holly spotted what looked like a sort of monorail with an old-fashioned navy blue pram perched on top of it. The pram wheels had been bent and curled, fastening it to the rail and the middle had been elongated. 'Its like a stretch limousine' said Cinnamon and with that the guinea pigs scampered aboard!

'This,' announced Mr Leafblower with tremendous pride, 'is my leaf flume. Let's go for a ride!' With one leap he too was in the pram.

Cautious but excited, the girls followed Cinnamon and Treacle and Mr Leafblower as they climbed into the pram. They were instructed to hold on tight as it began to slowly climb upwards.

'I never thought I'd be in a pram again!' said Victoria, but before anyone could reply, the pram picked up speed and it was too late to even take a breath - for at the top they gasped to see the monorail drop steeply before them, and then the track whirled and curled as far as the eye could see. Before they could contemplate any of this, their ride had begun and they swooped downwards at a hundred miles an hour, twisting and snaking right then left, then upside down, as they flew round a wide loop, and then another bigger loop -- and still on and on they went! Faster and still gaining speed, they entered a left-hand turn, and all screamed with a combination of terror and delight as they tore on up another mountain of rail to plummet down the other end. Glancing to her side, Holly wanted to laugh: She could see Cinnamon and Treacle, with all their long hair blown back, clinging on for dear life!

Eventually, they began to slow and gently stopped.

'That was the coolest ride ever!' cried Victoria, as she climbed out, still breathless. Realising they had arrived at a different place, Holly asked Mr Leafblower where they were.

Clearing his throat and pressing his shoulders back as if ready to make an important speech, as he seemed to do whenever he spoke, Mr Leafblower told the girls that they were actually three miles away from Firwood; and, saying no more, he then bounced forward and carefully opened a door similar to the one in the compost heap but yellow.

This door had been woven from hay.

Holly and Victoria peered outside, and to their utter astonishment and shock saw, only a few feet in front of them, a woman on a horse they both recognised!

Quickly pulling the door closed, they looked at one another.

'M-Mum!' stammered Holly, and the two girls began to laugh. They laughed and laughed and couldn't stop; Holly even rolled on the ground! It was so incredibly strange to have ended up at Pale Farm!

When they were truly exhausted by all their laughter, they peered out again and, sure enough, trotting round the very field that the door opened into was Mum riding

Hawk the horse! Then they, Mr Leafblower, and the guinea pigs all began to laugh too!

Next they were treated to some lovely peach juice and biscuits, produced from the endless leaf pockets in Mr Leafblower's jacket. They rode back on the leaf flume and found it to be just as exhilarating going back the other way!

At the end of the day, carrying their tired pets, Holly and Victoria waved goodbye to Mr Leafblower, who made them promise to visit often since they now knew where his door was.

Quickly, the girls ran into the house to have lunch. Their friend Tom was coming to play this afternoon and they were dying to tell him all about the leaf flume.

Chapter Seven

The Angry Greenlings

Tom listened, bright-eyed, as they told him of the adventure they had had that very morning.

'Ooh, please show me the leaf flume!' he pleaded, and the girls were easily persuaded, because they too were eager to revisit the grassy den beneath the compost heap.

Back down the metal ladder they went, this time with Tom in tow and also joined by Sooty the little black poodle.

'Look, Tom!' Holly said breathlessly, pointing ahead as the monorail came into view.

'Can we take a ride?' asked Tom.

'I'm not sure,' said Holly, hesitating, 'let's look around to see if we can find Mr Leafblower and ask.'

However, there was no reply when they called out Mr Leafblower's name, and Tom, who could resist no longer, climbed on board. The others quickly followed.

Holly was a little reluctant, and, inching in beside Sooty, whispered, 'Don't touch anything!'

'Listen,' whispered Sooty in return, who was so excited he could barely stop his little tail from wagging. Then they all heard it: a deep rumbling, and before they could do anything about it, the leaf flume began to move.

'Hang on tight!' shouted Victoria, her voice fading as they shot upwards like a bullet firing from a gun.

They all screamed as they momentarily glimpsed the very top and saw the incredible vertical drop ahead which they were soon whooshing down. On and on the pram carried them, careering left and then around a loop, and on they went just like before, except this time the leaf flume seemed to veer off down one of the many side tunnels and, without warning, it came to a juddering stop.

Hopping out, they could see they were in a narrower tunnel, which was darker than before.

Victoria spoke first, saying, 'I wonder where we are...'

'Sshh!' Tom interrupted her, having heard a strange noise. Standing together quietly they listened, and it sounded like lots of snoring!

Then they spotted it a large, green mound further down the tunnel.

'Let's take a look!' Sooty said, and bounded towards it. The children followed, though with a bit more caution

than their four-legged friend, who was sniffing and wagging all around it. As they got closer, they could make out that the mound was actually lots of separate round green balls, stacked together forming a sort of pyramid.

Each was about the size of a football, they looked as though they were made of thick blades of grass squashed together and they all seemed to be alive, asleep, and snoring! Before the children could warn Sooty to leave these creatures alone, he had begun to pull at one of these strange balls with his mouth.

He tugged and tugged until it rolled out of the pile and landed bump on the ground right in front of them. Immediately, two thick-set legs and arms shot out and a face could became visible on the tiny ball, with screwed-up eyes and a cross mouth. It was obvious that it was very angry. Within seconds, the whole pile had rolled apart; hidden arms and legs were flicked out, and hundreds of creatures stared at the children in a hostile manner.

Several of the round creatures marched towards the little gang of children and animals, looking quite unfriendly.

'We are the Greenlings and this is our tunnel. Why did you wake us?' they chanted together grumpily, staring first at Sooty, who could not resist a few barks, and then at the children.

'I'm very sorry,' stammered Holly, now afraid. 'We didn't mean to wake you. We are friends of Mr Leafblower and we took a ride on his leaf flume. I suppose it brought us down the wrong tunnel.'

'Why did you wake us?' they cried together again. 'We were very tired and we hate being woken!' As if in revenge, several of the Greenlings grabbed Sooty and began dragging him back down the tunnel.

Sooty gave out a yelp.

'Stop!' shouted Holly, and the others began to holler too, but it was all in vain. The Greenlings had pulled their arms and legs back into their round bodies and rolled down the tunnel, balancing the terrified Sooty on top of them.

'Hey!' yelled Tom, trying to catch up with them. 'You can't take our friend!' But they could no longer even make out the faintest outline as the Greenlings disappeared into the blackness of the long tunnel, taking dear, sweet Sooty with them as a prisoner.

The children looked at each other in disbelief.

'Ooh,' said Victoria rather huskily as she was trying not to get upset, 'What on earth shall we do now?'

'We must rescue him!' Holly said boldly, and, kneeling down, she began to empty her pockets, searching for anything that might help them in this task.

'You two check your pockets, too, in case there's anything we can use,' she instructed Victoria and Tom.

Victoria had only a piece of chewing gum and a paper hanky. Tom sheepishly revealed a halfeaten fudge and an old inky rubber. Holly sifted through her pockets in turn, which were full of all sorts of bits and pieces, until she felt something and pulled it out.

'Look,' she gasped with relief, 'surely this will help!' Holly held out the pale blue penfeather that she had been given by Mrs Mole at the Wampum festival. 'Remember what she said to us: 'Write wisely and you shall see me again'!'

With that, the three of them wrote a frantic note on Victoria's paper hanky.

Dear Madame Mole,

Help us please, our friend Sooty has been captured by angry Greenlings and we are lost in one of the tunnels beneath the compost heap. Our friend Mr Leafblower doesn't even know we are here!

Quickly, they all signed their names; and before Holly had even folded the note, a beautiful giant brown moth with shiny blue-green circles on its wings, like those on a peacock's feathers appeared, hovering beside them. Gently it swooped and carefully lifted the note from Holly's hands, and was gone in a flash.

'I suppose we'll just have to wait now,' said Tom, but Victoria jumped to her feet.

'We must go down the tunnel and see if we can find where they have taken him! We must!' she almost shouted, newly moved by poor Sooty's plight.

Holly agreed; she knew they must do something, for there was no guarantee that their note would even be received.

'You're right,' said Tom, 'perhaps the lazy Greenlings

are sleeping again, further down the tunnel.'

At once, all three of them began to edge their way through the darkness. Hesitating at each curve, they sneaked quietly on, hoping they would not meet the enemy head on or walk into a trap. Victoria's hand trembled as it clung to her sister's, and Tom thought that his chest would nearly burst with his heart beating so loudly. Even though they were frightened the determined gang edged their way along.

As they carried on down the dark tunnel Holly shivered, wondering what the Greenlings were capable of and why she had even agreed to pursue them in the first place.

Too late! She saw it at the same time as the others - something moving ahead and blocking their path,and worse, what ever it was now advancing towards them!

Bracing themselves for trouble, the children now came face to face with... Madame Mole! Breathing sighs of relief, they embraced their old friend.

Chapter Eight

Saving Sooty

Tom was fascinated as he watched the huge figure that loomed ahead of them shrink in seconds into a small creature the size of a cat. Looking closely he could see that this was actually a rather large mole: Madame Mole, he guessed. She extended her paw and shook his hand. She can change size whenever she wanted too, just like the girls had said happened at the Wampum festival, thought Tom, as he felt the warmth of her fingers grasp his.

The children knelt down beside Madame Mole and hastily recounted what had taken place, how they had met Mr Leafblower and become his friend and ridden with him on his leaf flume. They told her, with some embarrassment, how they had foolishly ridden the leafflume by themselves, and finally how, worst of all, Sooty had been taken away by the strange creatures called Greenlings.

Madame Mole listened with her head tilted to one side, and when the children had finished she began to speak in her soft voice, her bright eyes gleaming light into the darkness of the tunnel.

'The Greenlings have lived in the eastern tunnel for a very long time, over a million years.' She spoke quietly, almost in a whisper for fear of being heard. 'And, as I am afraid you have already found out, they do not respond well to visitors – or as they see them, intruders. Especially those who do what Greenlings hate most of all.'

Unsure as to what she meant, Tom asked, 'What do they hate most of all?'

'Being woken, Tom,' she continued. 'They are unfriendly and grumpy by nature, and losing sleep because they have been woken by anyone or anything is to them a great offence. As indeed is entering the eastern tunnel without their invitation! In these circumstances I do not believe we will be able to persuade them to release your little friend.'

The children were aware of the very serious tone of her voice. Vikki groaned, and Madame Mole spoke more urgently now.

'Greenlings do not give back anything they find in their tunnel, therefore we must try to rescue Sooty quickly before they move on. They travel at great speed and their tunnel is hundreds of miles long. Once on the move we will not be able to catch them, they roll together as a group and do not stop for many days.' Pausing, she then added quietly, 'I hope we are not too late.'

With that, Madame Mole stood and blew silently upwards. Almost at once a colourful moth appeared and landed at her side.

The news the moth brought was encouraging: the Greenlings had stopped about two hundred metres further down the tunnel. But there was some bad news too: Sooty had been tied by a length of rope to one of the Greenlings who slept at the base of their newly formed pyramid. He too was fast asleep, drugged it seemed by a drink of the Greenlings' water that the thirsty little dog had lapped up.

Holly could hardly contain her anger: 'How dare they!' she hissed, 'Sooty only wanted to play, how cruel they are! We must sneak back down the tunnel and cut the rope immediately!'

'Unfortunately my guess is that the rope is made of greling, which the Greenlings spin themselves. It is very strong and, I have heard tell, unbreakable.'

Madame Mole sighed but then, lifting her head, she added, 'But you are right, young Holly, we must first try.'

The small party made their way back down the tunnel towards where they now knew their enemy to be sleeping. Sure enough, as they pressed themselves close to the tunnel wall and gingerly rounded the second bend, they saw the Greenlings stacked in the same pyramid shape as when they had first come across these strange beings. And there was Sooty, almost hidden in the dark of the tunnel, camouflaged by his black curly coat and tethered to a Greenling, just as the moth had said. Without a word to the others, Madame Mole crept forward, shrinking as she did so to the size of a mouse, and on reaching the greling rope she began to gnaw as fast as she could. Again and again she attacked the rope with her razor-sharp teeth but to no avail. The greling rope was, as she suspected, unbreakable, and eventually she had to admit defeat and return, having made no impact on the rope at all. With a sigh, she whispered to the children what they had already guessed:

'The greling rope will not give.'

Just then, she and the others heard a noise. The pile suddenly moved, and the snoring was interrupted. The children gasped; there was no time to waste, the Greenlings were getting restless and could wake any time now. If they did, the consequences wouldn't even bear thinking about.

Luckily, Madame Mole was struck with a new idea. Once again she blew into the air, and the moth swooped down beside her. This time she reached under one of his velvet-like wings and pulled out a small bag. Inside it was a glass jar with a gold top, which she deftly unscrewed. Quickly, she was once again at Sooty's side, and they saw a tiny yellow speck of dust from the jar land on Sooty. Just in time, too!

Sooty seemed to disappear to the children, who were struggling to see in the dim light of the tunnel. The next thing they knew, Madame Mole was back beside them and, to their amazement, carrying a miniature Sooty, who she had been able to slip through the rope that had tied him!

'He won't remain small for long, so we must leave at once. Run!' ordered Madame Mole, and the children turned and sped as fast as they could back up the tunnel; as did Madame Mole, who was carrying the tiny sleeping dog in her arms.

Whether it was the noise of their running that woke

the sleeping pyramid they did not know, but behind them the children and their companions could clearly hear a commotion as the pile flew apart and the Greenlings realised that Sooty had gone!

Faster and faster Holly and the others ran, but as they did they heard the rumble of many Greenlings rolling after them. A quick glance backwards meant that Vikki saw the first row of Greenlings only metres away, waving their fists and screaming, 'Bring back our toy, bring back our toy! Finders keepers, losers weepers!'

Tom felt that his legs would give way and that he could run no further, but the sound of Madame Mole ahead encouraged him to press on and helped him pick up his pace in a final push for freedom.

Just when it seemed they would surely be caught, they saw in the distance someone beckoning and waving to them, and with great joy they realised it was their friend Mr Leafblower on board his leaf flume.

'Climb on board!' he roared towards them, 'hurry, dear friends, hurry!'

He was standing at the front of the flume and they could hear the hum of the engine, knowing that if only they could reach it they could be gone like a flash.

Holly reached it first and dived into a seat, dragging her sister behind her, then Madame Mole with her precious black package... but where was Tom?

Looking back, Holly gasped. Tom was running breathlessly, but behind him by only a stride were the Greenlings.

'Run, Tom, run, run!' shouted Holly.

Then she noticed something else: a large row of lights set out along the ground. These were the car headlights that had previously lit up Mr Leafblower's grassy den. They were set up in a line only a short distance away from the vehicle and - oh my goodness - sat on top of the middle light was Monty!

Now they heard Tom cry out, and the girls watched in horror as one of the Greenlings reached out and grabbed at him. It grasped his T-shirt and, jerking backwards, Tom nearly fell, but regained his footing as he heard the unmistakable voice of Monty call out to him.

'Only a few more steps, Tom, and you're safe!'

With virtually his last ounce of strength Tom pulled away, passing the lights and heading for his friends.

As soon as he passed the row of lights, Monty pressed a switch and all at once the lights came on. With the unexpected blast of illumination aimed right at them the Greenlings were momentarily stunned, and like a train hitting a wall they crashed into each other, bouncing and skidding along the ground.

Before they had chance to recover, Monty had shouted the order, and the leaf flume was gone faster (it seemed to the children) than it had ever gone. The friends were whisked off back up the track and in what seemed like only a few seconds they realised the leaf flume was back where they had found it that very first time, and that they were all safe. Monty had been the last to leap to safety, landing beside Mr Leafblower the very second they sped away.

Sitting in Mr Leafblower's den beneath the compost heap, they chatted about their great adventure. As they passed around the tac flowers that tasted of different flavours of ice-cream and drank the raspberry juice doled out by Cinnamon and Treacle, they could hardly believe how close they had come to losing their canine friend and possibly Tom as well. How refreshed they felt, and how glad they were to be back in the magic garden!

Sooty wagged his tail with delight as he thanked his friends for rescuing him, and Monty and Mr Leafblower made the children promise never to ride the leaf flume without them again, to which they all readily agreed!

Glancing at his watch, Tom saw that it was getting late and that his Mum would soon be arriving at the house to take him home. He too wanted everyone to make a promise: that he could come and play again and find out more about the magic of the garden. Once again, everyone agreed.

As the girls snuggled down to sleep that night, they couldn't help but wonder what or who they would meet next in the garden. What they didn't know then was that it had all just begun, and that lots of new adventures were due to take place at Firwood very, very soon!

Chapter Nine

Tom Disappears

A loud meow caught Holly's attention and she saw immediately that Monty meant her to follow as he padded downstairs.

Vikki had not heard Monty, though seeing the others disappear past her bedroom door she too decided to find out what was going on, even though it was early, something exciting was likely to happen if Monty was involved!

The snap and clunk of the front door being opened confirmed they were headed into the garden and Vikki could feel butterflies gathering in her stomach because she knew that that meant there was a good chance that another adventure was about to begin in the magic garden.

Both girls followed as Monty led them outside. Passing a row of little fat lavender bushes, they found themselves in a secret part of the garden that they had not seen before. This was not unusual and the children had become accustomed to surprises like this, living in such a magic place.

Here, a square room filled with shrubs was defined by three chunky dark green hedges which surrounded a pond. A blaze of tall blue, red and yellow flowers filled the borders.

Sitting on the pond wall, Monty's eyes sparked as he began to speak to them about these flowery giants called lupins.

'They're about to puff!' he said, with a cat grin, 'and when they do, be sure you are nowhere near or you may find yourselves in trouble!'

'What do you mean, puff?' cried the girls.

As the sun was hot and the temperature rising, Monty hopped down from the pond wall and positioned himself in the cool shade of the softly swaying flowers. The girls followed and plonked down beside him, and he continued: 'The lupins very rarely puff out their trumpets of flowers, but when they do, dive for cover quick! For even the tiniest speck of lupin dust will shrink any living thing for days.'

And with that he began licking his paw as if he hadn't said anything amazing at all. But the girls were amazed, and had already begun to talk about what might happen when the lupins puffed.

'Shrinking!' said Vikki, thinking out loud.

'Monty, how shrunk do you mean?' asked Holly. Realising how funny that sounded, she laughed, and Vikki and Monty laughed too.

'Very shrunk,' Monty replied smartly.

So it was that the children learnt about the tall flowers called lupins, and began daily trips to that part of the garden hoping to see the results of such an event, or maybe even to witness it. After all, it could be quite exciting to see lots of garden flowers blow their flowery heads off, let alone a mouse or passing bird become a miniature version of themselves. *Could it really happen?* they wondered.

A whole week passed and nothing had happened. Tom came to stay on Saturday night, heard all about the puffing flowers and ran to see for himself, but they just tossed their flowery heads in the wind and didn't seem strange to him at all.

Tom played hide and seek with Claudia and Barry the squirrels until bedtime, forgetting all about the lupins and their shrinking powers. They were all tired after a busy sunny day in the magic garden and fell asleep quickly.

Holly woke in a daze to find Monty pulling and pawing at her quilt. A short sharp meow left her in no doubt that she was to come at once, and, grabbing her dressing gown, she left her bedroom and followed her friend.

Next they stopped at the spare room and woke Tom, signaling for him to follow, and with combined efforts woke Vikki, which actually took quite a bit of prodding!

As all three of them reached the bottom of the stairs, they began to hear noises. At first, they had no idea what it was so they cautiously moved towards the kitchen, and the noises got louder and more familiar. Birdsong mixed with what sounded like the squeaking of mice and all sorts of other animal speak seemed to fill the air.

Even this didn't prepare them for what they saw when they actually opened the door that led from the hall into the kitchen. The whole floor, every inch of it, was covered with the birds and animals from the magic garden! The wood pigeons were on the kitchen bench and two small greenfinches were swinging on the copper pans Mum had hung from hooks above the sink.

Amongst all of this, Vikki could just make out Barry and Claudia, the twin squirrels, who were sitting near the back door, squashed between a family of grey rabbits.

The sound of the cat flap continued to slap open and closed as every few minutes, more animals came through and edged into any available space they could find. Soon

the floor was no longer visible, and every other available surface held an array of little creatures, including several groups of quite big snails!

'What on earth has happened, Monty?' stammered Tom, trying to take it all in. The girls were still far too surprised to say anything!

'Me.ow,' answered their furry friend – and with that they remembered they would have to unlock the back door and go outside into the magic garden to talk to him. At once, they made their way outside and into the velvety black of the night, where a splash of light from the moon gilded the fur of Monty's coat and he told them what Holly and Vikki had already suspected.

'The lupins have just puffed, and while the air still has lupin dust in it, the animals are finding shelter wherever they can. There are lots of hazards when you find yourself suddenly the size of a petal or a peppercorn! I called out to everyone to follow me through the cat flap.' He spoke quietly so as not to wake the sleeping adults.

'By dawn, the dust will have settled and all the animals will leave the kitchen. Your parents won't even know they have had any nocturnal visitors!'

After a slight pause he added, 'Well.. I hope not,' and beamed his cheeky smile at them.

There was silence for a moment while the three children processed this information.

Then Tom said 'I want to see!' and before anyone could dissuade him, he had dashed towards where he knew the lupins grew.

Immediately, Monty careered after him, swiftly followed by Holly and Victoria. But at the entrance to the little enclave where the pond sat and the lupins grew, Monty stopped and, leaping in front, prevented the girls from entering.

'It's too dangerous,' he husked. 'Tom has been very foolish; we may not see him for days! We can only hope he can stay safe because he may well be the size of a tiny pea or even smaller, depending on how much dust touched him.'

To confirm what he had just said, Monty shimmied up the nearest tree and peered into the black of the night. Tom was not there, or more accurately, too small to be seen anymore, even by the eyes of a cat.

Tom felt a strange sensation; it was as if a ball of energy had been fired into him, warming him from the inside out, and it made him want to giggle. Then a fierce blast of wind swept him off his feet.

Landing on what initially seemed like a ploughed grey field of soil, he knew for certain he had been well and truly shrunk!

From the light of a dull half-crescent moon he could see the jungle of swaying lupin trees all around. About a metre in front of him, what would have been small pebbles formed a wall of boulders.

He heard now another noise in the distant dark - a rustle of branches perhaps, but he was unsure. What Tom did not know was that it was indeed a rustle of branches, for Monty was now at the top of a tree looking for any sign of his young friend.

A sudden bout of shrieks, coupled with the flapping

of seemingly hundreds of wings, jolted Tom, making him cower and move closer behind the boulders for cover. Just in time! Because now, above him, he could hear and see a swirling flock of bats, menacing in comparison to his tiny size.

Could they be predators now he wondered. Tom's heart pounded like a drum, and he was relieved when the noise of the bats stopped as they moved away. Then there was only the sound of the trees.

I must find out where I am, he thought, and so cautiously he began to cross the field. He certainly didn't recognise this part of the garden.

After an hour or so, he came to a wall of pinkish red. As he peered over the edge of the wall he could see it was a sheer drop to the ground below, at least fifteen feet and too far for him to jump. All at once, he realised where he was. He was inside a plant pot and had reached what would have been the rim!

Sitting down, tired after his journey, Tom wondered if the others had also been touched by the dust. Were they somewhere close? He shouted their names several times, but no one answered.

After a while, he was woken by footsteps and knew that he must have fallen asleep. He had no idea of the time but guessed that it must be morning and was grateful for the daylight.

'Tom! Tom!' the girls were shouting in the garden. Hearing them call his name, he leapt to his feet and called back to them. He desperately wanted to be found now, so that he could show them how tiny he was, and he certainly didn't want to be alone outside for another night. The girls of course didn't hear as his voice was so quiet, but Tom heard their footsteps fade as they searched elsewhere, and heard Vikki say, 'It was selfish of Tom to run off like that.'

Holly replied, 'It doesn't matter now, we have to find him before he gets trampled or hurt.'

Tom missed his friends and knew what they said was true.

A feeling of something watching him made Tom turn around and he saw that a giant robin had fixed its round eye on him. It was perched on the wooden handle of a spade that had been left upright in the soil, and had a hungry look.

At the same time, he realised he was not alone anymore in the plant pot. Close to him, a ladybird had landed, and Tom was only just bigger than one of her black spots! She was incredibly shiny, like red nail polish, and nodded in his direction as a way of saying hello.

After telling him her name (Libby Ladybird), she asked him why he only had two legs.

Tom laughed. 'I'm not an insect,' he said 'actually I'm a boy and I got caught in the lupin dust. Normally I'm four foot eight!'

The two chatted happily for a few minutes, forgetting all about the robin, until they both heard the noise of its wings beating and felt a gush of air close to them. Without warning, the robin had flown towards them and seemed to be mumbling something about breakfast. And in the next second they both realised that they were the most likely candidates!

The robin swooped and pecked at Libby. Immediately Tom saw that his new friend was about to be eaten and it was very likely that he might be pudding. He knew he must do something at once.

'Don't you dare try to eat my friend, you horrid robin!' Tom shouted. But the Robin didn't seem to hear; Tom was so small his voice had been reduced to a faint squeaking.

Libby threw out her tiny wings in an attempt to save herself so that she could fly away, but the bird's flapping wings above made it impossible.

Tom gasped in horror as the robin pecked again at his friend, and grabbing the only thing available - handfuls

of soil he began throwing them towards the robin. The giant bird now landed right beside them and with one last effort Tom threw soil directly at its eye, which succeeded in momentarily catching it off guard.

'Quick, Tom!' shouted Libby, 'Climb on my back!' and then they were airborne.

Smooth and deftly, Libby flew down into the long grass and weaved in and out of these green posts, leaving an angry and hungry robin behind.

Libby eventually landed gently on a grassy mound and Tom, who had slid down her glass-like back, found himself in what Libby told him was the land of the ladybirds. He would be safe here, she promised.

The ladybirds fussed around Tom; they had never seen anything this small with only two legs. Libby recounted what had happened to them in the plant pot, and they gasped out loud when the robin was mentioned. Then a whisper began among the little crowd, speaking of words that had been passed down through the ladybirds for generations. Had the prophecy come true?

They insisted that this was not a robin at all, but the Kloggerfwin with the long ferocious beak and that their friends may have been very lucky indeed. Libby explained to Tom that there was a boy in the ancient ladybird poem.

Tom was confused and, though he tried his hardest to tell them it had truly been a robin in the plant pot, the ladybirds were adamant that it must have been the Kloggerfwin, so he sat down with them and listened to their ancient poem so that he could decide for himself.

The leader of the ladybirds had hushed them all and began to recite the poem, while Tom listened, wide-eyed.

The Kloggerfwin with the Long Terocious Beak

.

Come to my knee
Dear frickle boy
And I shall tell you tales
Of ladybirds and gogleymins and deremints and whales

It was an oddly gribsous day
The sonnebrim shone bright
And it was such an undisturbed moggleichichu night
But not too quiet for the Kloggerfwin
With the long ferocious beak
To go searching for ladybirds
And other fresh meat

So bolt the door and arm the guns
And sim the brillery
For the Kloggerfwin is out and he might want you or me!
Run, oh run, calhobble, shun
Save yourself from he
Take my briggle, take my gun
And then just leave me!

And how the frickle boy he ran
But all in fraujus vain
For the Kloggerfwin is very quick and up the pot he came

The frickle boy, threw soil
Then flew by ladybird seat
And pursuing him the Kloggerfwin
With the long ferocious beak

So take my word, and take it well
Obey my quibbish word
Not to Crit the Kloggerfwin
You small gogiplog ladybirds

The ladybirds all stood at the end of the poem and clapped politely. Some of the older ones pulled smoking pipes from under their wings afterwards, and sat on pebbles together, discussing whether Libby and Tom had nearly been eaten by a Kloggerfwin.

Soon, Tom felt quite at home. He was tucking into a chunk of lady-bread and busy playing spot-the-spot with the Libby and her friends, when something strange began to happen to him.

The warm inside feeling was back and, once again, he was knocked off his feet by it. This time, though, Tom found that he had grown a little and that he was now at least six inches tall: far bigger than his newly -found friends.

'The lupin dust must be wearing off!' he shouted in a delighted voice. 'Surely now my friends will be able to see me!'

Waving goodbye, he left the land of the ladybirds, promising to visit again, and walked back in the direction of the pond, hoping to find the others. As he ambled along, he tried to remember the ladybird poem so he could tell the girls all about it.

Meanwhile, the girls had just about given up the search and had found it quite a challenge to keep pretending to their Mum that Tom was somewhere else in the garden every time she came to find them! It was difficult enough pretending that they had no idea why the kitchen was full of tiny feathers.

It was Monty, with his keen hearing, that heard a little voice in the distance and knew immediately it must be Tom.

'This way!' he hollered, and Holly and Vikki followed and there, at the edge of a neatly paved path, stood Tom.

Tom climbed onto the hand offered by Holly and apologised for the muddiness of his shoes. The children took turns to tell each other what had happened to them, with Tom yelling as loud as he could, and even then, they could only just hear him.

'You do look funny like that, Tom,' said Vikki, smiling and relieved that they had found him. 'How exciting to ride on the back of a ladybird!'

Before Tom had time to answer, he felt the curious warm sensation again, and the next thing he knew was that he was half his original size.

'Take cover!' Monty shouted, because just as Tom had grown, Mum had appeared, calling that lunch was ready. Tom reappeared from behind the lavender bush when she had gone.

'Whatever shall we do now?' said Vikki, looking first at Monty and then at Holly. In the distance, they heard Mum calling them again for lunch.

'We have to go in,' said Holly, 'and we will have to say that we have lost Tom again!'

'Oh no!' groaned Vikki, 'We really will be in trouble now!'.

The girls headed back towards the house, to the sound of Tom's voice behind them, shouting, 'Save me something, I'm really hungry!'

However, they were in for a pleasant surprise. Just as they had finished washing their hands and sat down at the table, a smiling Tom walked through the back door, completely back to his normal size. What a relief! They didn't need to pretend at all.

In fact, everything was back to normal... Well, that is, it was until the next adventure in Firwood the magic garden which was not far away!

FIRWOOD

The Magic Garden

Written By

LYNNE ARMSTRONG-HOBBS

FIRWOOD

The Magic Garden

I would like to thank Holly Armstrong for her patience and support

The use of first four lines of the poem by W.B Yeats - page 30.